W9-ASX-586

CHICKEN
IN THE MIDDLE
OF THE ROAD

For Matthew and Amy, and all the chickens that have ever fallen off the back of a truck — I.R.

This edition first published in the United States in 1997 by
MONDO Publishing
By arrangement with MULTIMEDIA INTERNATIONAL (UK) LTD

Text copyright © 1987 by Ian Renwick
Illustrations copyright © 1987 by Margie Chellew

All rights reserved.
No part of this publication may be reproduced, except in the case of quotation for articles or reviews, or stored in any retrieval system, or transmitted in any form or by any means, electronic, mechanical, photocopying, recording, or otherwise, without written permission from the publisher.

For information contact:
MONDO Publishing
980 Avenue of the Americas
New York, NY 10018

Printed in Hong Kong
First Mondo printing, October 1996

01 02 03 04 05   9 8 7 6 5 4

ISBN 1-57255-189-5

Originally published in Australia in 1987 by Horwitz Publications Pty Ltd
Original development by Robert Andersen & Associates and Snowball Educational

Chicken
in the Middle
of the Road

by Ian Renwick
Illustrated by Margie Chellew

MONDO

One morning, as the sun rose, a truck came along the Tooradin Road.

The driver turned up the heater and listened to the radio as he drove along.

He didn't notice something fall off the back of the truck.

A little while later, two men were going
to work and they saw some white ruffled
feathers in the middle of the road.

The driver was in a hurry, so he kept going.

As the sun climbed above the trees,
Debbie Watson passed the white ruffled
feathers on her way to school.

Oh *yuk*! A *dead chicken*, she thought.
Debbie Watson kept on walking.

Two friends, Barry and Ian, were not far from school when they heard the bell ring.

"Hey, Barry. Look at the dead chicken!" shouted Ian.

They walked over to it. Barry bent down and prodded the chicken with his finger.

"It's still alive," he announced. "Quick, lend me your sweater."

There was blood on the chicken's head and it didn't try to run away when Barry wrapped it up in Ian's sweater.

When they got to school, everyone was already inside.

"Sorry we're late, Mrs. Wills," said Barry, "but we had to stop and help this."

Some of the children looked up as Barry started to unfold the sweater.

"Oh yuk," squealed Debbie Watson. "It's the dead chicken from the middle of the road!"

Everyone stopped what they were doing and tried to get a closer look.

Mrs. Wills sent Barry and Ian to find a box for the chicken. They also brought back a container for some water and a cracker from Ian's lunch.

They left the chicken near the window in the classroom.

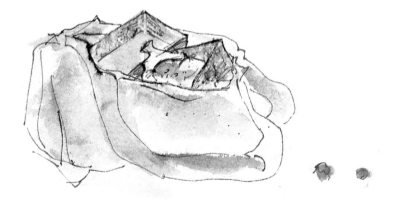

At lunchtime, Barry and Ian were allowed
to stay inside. They sat in the corridor
and tried to feed the chicken some soggy
cracker crumbs.

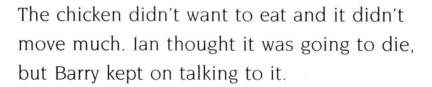

The chicken didn't want to eat and it didn't
move much. Ian thought it was going to die,
but Barry kept on talking to it.

After school Barry and Ian carried the chicken
home in the box. All the kids kept wanting to
look at it.

When they reached Barry's house, Barry's little sister Jemima was playing in the front yard.

When Jemima saw what was in the box she raced inside shouting, "A cockadoo! A cockadoo!"

Barry's mom came out and looked in the
box. Barry and Ian told her the whole story.

"You'd better bring it inside for tonight," she
said, "but just for tonight."

Within a few days the new "cockadoo" began
to eat and flap its wings. Soon it hopped out
of the box and began to explore the backyard.

Two weeks later Barry's mom was looking out the kitchen window. She turned to Barry and smiled.

"Your chicken from the middle of the road seems quite happy being a chicken in the middle of the yard," she said.

Well, sometimes.